A FOREST CHRISTMAS

A Forest Christmas

by Mayling Mack Holm

Harper & Row, Publishers
New York, Hagerstown, San Francisco, London

Library of Congress Cataloging in Publication Data
Holm, Mayling Mack.
    A forest Christmas.

    SUMMARY: The forest animals gather at
Mrs. Rabbit's house for a Christmas Eve celebration.
    [1. Christmas stories.   2. Forest animals—
Fiction] I. Title.
PZ7.H7323Fo   [E]   76-58696
ISBN 0-06-022572-6
ISBN 0-06-022573-4 lib. bdg.

To Kim, Jenny, and Darcy

A FOREST CHRISTMAS

It is Christmas Eve in the forest. Tonight all of the animals are invited to a party at Mrs. Rabbit's house.

In the Oak Tree, the littlest squirrel is napping. Soon his mother will wake him with a surprise. She is wearing a Christmas crown of candles and bringing him hot chocolate and a sweet bun.

The mouse family has the busiest house in the forest because there are so many mice! But two clever mice have found a quiet spot by a window. They want to see how many snowflakes they can count before putting on their party clothes.

At the rat household, everyone is dressed and ready to go. They are just finishing their eggnog while Mrs. Rat is choosing a special Christmas hat to wear to the party.

Now all the animals are on their way,
hurrying to the house in the center of the
woods. They can see the lights in the win-
dows and smell the good food that Mrs.
Rabbit is cooking.

Mrs. Rabbit stands by her door and welcomes everyone. She gives the youngest rat a hug and a scratch behind his ear.

The children sit together at their own tables. After eating all their favorite foods, they give each other presents, and Father Mouse lights their dessert—a Christmas pudding.

On this special night, all the children stay up past their bedtime, listening to their parents singing Christmas carols.

The little rabbit and the mouse put on their puppet show. Everyone laughs at the clown and the bear, but they laugh most of all at Father Rabbit. He is wearing silly clothes and helping by playing the fiddle, but he doesn't know how!

It is very dark and very late. Mrs. Rabbit turns out all the lamps, and a hush falls over the room as she lights the last candle on the Christmas tree.

Everyone is quiet. Christmas Eve is almost over, and there's just enough time for the children to hear the Christmas story. And then . . .

it is Christmas!

Typography by Kohar Alexanian
Set in Goudy Old Style
Composed by Royal Composing Room
Printed by Thomas Todd Company
Bound by Publishers Book Bindery
Harper & Row, Publishers, Incorporated